Please, Just Leave the Glass

Written by Santa Paul

Illustrated by Elisha Gillette

Visit our website at www.StillwaterPress.com for more information.

First Stillwater River Publications Edition

ISBN: 978-1-960505-75-0

Library of Congress Control Number: 2023917983

Names: Santa Paul, author. | Gillette, Elisha, illustrator.
Title: Please, just leave the glass / written by Santa Paul ; illustrated by Elisha Gillette.
Description: First Stillwater River Publications edition. | West Warwick, RI, USA : Stillwater River
Publications, [2023] | Audience: Juvenile.
Identifiers: ISBN: 978-1-960505-75-0 | LCCN: 2023917983
Subjects: LCSH: Santa Claus (Fictitious character)—Juvenile fiction. | Girls—Juvenile fiction. | Likes
    and dislikes—Juvenile fiction. | Christmas stories. | CYAC: Santa Claus (Fictitious character)—
    Fiction. | Girls—Fiction. | Likes and dislikes—Fiction. | Christmas—Fiction. | LCGFT: Christmas
    fiction.
Classification: LCC: PZ7.1.S26324 Pl 2023 | DDC: [E]—dc2

1 2 3 4 5 6 7 8 9 10

Written by Paul Evans.
Illustrated and designed by Elisha Gillette.
Published by Stillwater River Publications, West Warwick, RI, USA.

This book is dedicated to my beatiful, amazing grandchildren: Juliet (7), Darcy (5),
Evan (5), Heath (3), Ben (2), Conrad (2),
and twin angels in heaven, John Robert and
Thomas Francis.

Love Always and Forever,
Papa HoHo

*I*t's Christmas Eve! I've hung the stockings, decorated the tree, and sprinkled reindeer food in the yard. Everything is ready, even the milk and cookies.

But I can't sleep!

My mind is racing.

Did Santa get my list? Is it too long? Am
I on the "nice list" or not? Will I get a
puppy, a dream camper, a pink Cadillac, or
a unicorn?

There's no way I can sleep thinking about
all this stuff!

Suddenly, I hear a noise.

What's that? Is it Rudolph on the roof?
Is it an elf? Is it Santa?

I lie in bed wondering what I should do
until I can't take it anymore.

I've got to go investigate!

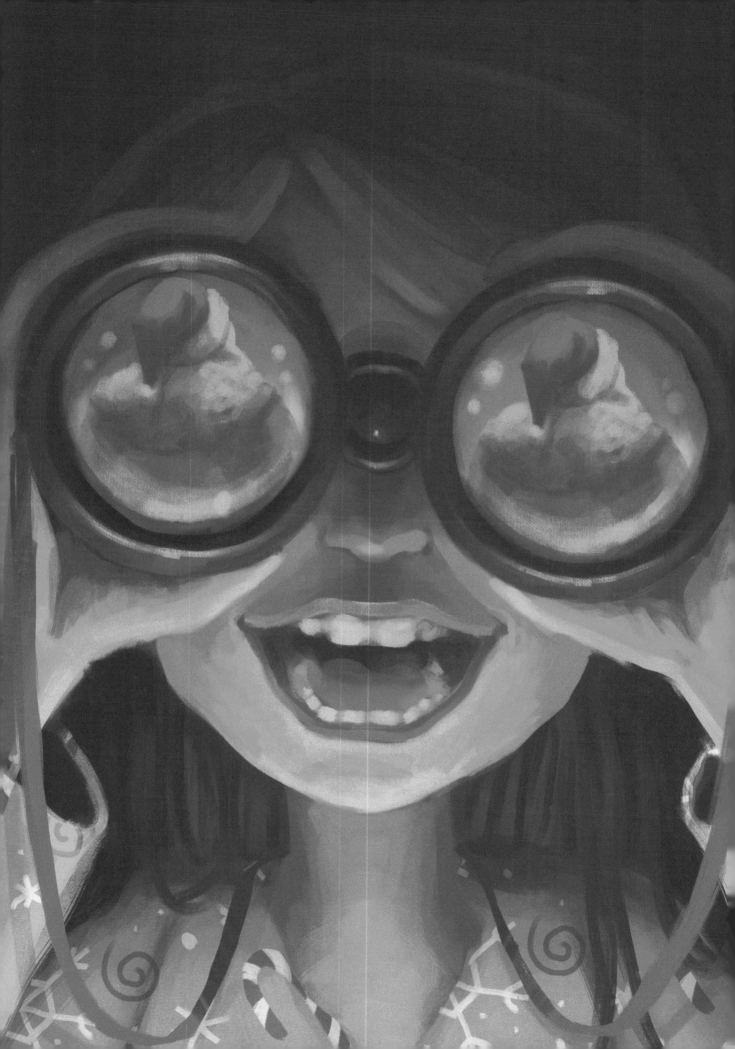

I turn the corner, and there he is.
Santa is standing in MY kitchen!

He's taller than I thought, with twinkling
eyes and cheeks that look like roses. Even
his nose is red like a cherry. And that long
white beard? It's as white as snow!

Santa is holding the special glass of milk with his name on it. Then I can't believe my eyes—he pours the glass of milk down the kitchen sink!

I gasp, and he turns to see me.

Uh oh! I try to hide, but I'm too late.

"Hello," Santa says. He sits on a chair and motions me over.

I can't move. My feet are frozen!

"Come sit with me. It's okay," Santa says.

Somehow my feet are walking, and I can't believe I'm standing in front of the real Santa!

"So, you want a puppy, eh?" he says with twinkling eyes. "You know they're a lot of work, right?"

I don't answer and just nod.

Santa smiles down at me. "Mrs. Claus and Santa have made a new rule. It's simple. If you want a puppy or really any live animal like a cat, hamster, ferret, or pony...you know what the rule is?"

I shake my head. I'm still in awe that he is really here.

"You don't know the rule?" he asks smiling. "Well, I always tell kids...ask the Easter Bunny!" He laughs so hard it fills the kitchen. "HO! HO! HO!"

I manage to smile even though I'm so nervous.

"The truth is," Santa says, "not only is it too cold on the sleigh, but families need to pick out their own pets together and not have Santa do it. Isn't that a good rule?"

"I guess so," I say, finally getting the courage to smile.

We sit and talk and talk! We talk about flying reindeer and magic keys (for the houses that don't have chimneys...who knew?). I learn all about the silly elves, Elfie, Chippy, Snowflake, Jingles, and Buddy, and even Santa's own house elves, Eddie Spaghetti and Charlie Horse!

Santa has A LOT to say about the elves! "I always tell them... remember what you learned in Elf School," he says. "I say, 'stay away from the bathroom and ceiling fans!' But do they listen?" Santa throws up his hands in frustration. "Just last week, I had thirteen unlucky elves get hurt. People turn on their ceiling fan and WOO WOO, they go flying!"

After a while, Santa asks about my report card and if I'm studying hard in school. We talk about keeping my hands to myself and playing nice with others. We even talk about keeping my room clean and doing my chores cheerfully. He asks if I'm a good listener and a good helper.

"I sure am," I say.

"And you're cutting back on the attitude and drama?" he asks with a wink.

Ooh, I knew that was coming!

Santa just smiles. "You'll be okay," he says. "But my, oh my, look at the time! I have so much to do before Christmas morning!"

Santa gets up and sends me off to bed.

"Okay, Santa," I say, "I'll go, but can I just ask two more questions?"

Santa nods. "Sure, go for it!"

"What is your favorite cookie?"

"Oh, that's an easy one...round!" Santa says as he belts out a big "HO! HO! HO!" Then he looks serious. "The truth is I love homemade chocolate chip cookies, but I do get lots of them, so I like a nice variety. I'm really not too fussy when it comes to cookies. But please don't forget a snack for the reindeer. They love apples, oats, carrots, and even cold pizza or mac n' cheese. Just like me! HO! HO! HO!"

Santa and the reindeer like mac n' cheese? Who knew?

I turn to leave when I suddenly remember my most important question of all. "Why did you pour the glass of milk down the drain?"

"Oh no, you saw me? Hmm, well, the truth is...do you like warm milk?"

"Warm milk? Yuck! I even put ice cubes in my milk so it's nice and cold! I can't stand warm milk!" I say.

"Me too!" Santa says. "See, most of the milk I get has been sitting out for hours and hours and it gets really warm. BLECH!"

Santa rubs his belly. "I'm old, and warm milk doesn't agree with my belly anymore. Even though I do have a little magic, I can't do everything. You see, I can make reindeer fly, I have a magic door key, and I can even deliver presents all in one night. But for the life of me…I can't change warm milk to be cold again!" he laughs. "But I am a big boy, and I know how to open the refrigerator, get the milk out, and pour it myself. So next year…" Santa pauses,

"Please, just leave the glass."

I laugh. Imagine, all this time I've been pouring milk and really, Santa wanted to do it himself. Who knew?

The End

Acknowledgements

A very special thank you to my brother firefighters, brother Santas, former students, and friends and family—all who have helped me through this MAGICAL journey. I am especially grateful to Elisha Gillette for their amazing illustrations and not making Santa too "chubby and plump." And lastly, I am eternally grateful to Mrs. Claus for always being by my side!

About the Star

Juliet is a second grader from Northbridge, Massachusetts. She loves school and wants to be a teacher someday. She also very much loves her family—especially her little brothers Evan and Ben. Juliet is involved in Girl Scouts, CCD, swimming, soccer, and gymnastics, and her favorite time of year is Christmas. She loves to watch Disney movies; her favorite is *Godmothered*, starring her own Papa HoHo!

About the Author

SANTA PAUL EVANS is a real bearded, real belly, professional Santa Claus from Rhode Island. He is a graduate of the International University of Santa Claus and a member of the Northeast, New England, and Connecticut Santa Societies.

He can be seen (along with Mrs. Claus, his wife Peggy of 44 years) around Rhode Island, Massachusetts, and Connecticut visiting schools, daycares, nursing homes, businesses, and private parties. He is the official Santa for the Rhode Island State House Christmas Tree Lighting Ceremony with the Governor of Rhode Island.

He is a retired Physical Education teacher (St. Peter School, 34 years), a retired Lieutenant/EMT with the City of Warwick Fire Department, and a graduate of URI '77. They have two children, Justine and Michael, and six grandchildren.

🔊 www.santapaulri.com | www.justleavetheglass.com | ✉ santapaulri@gmail.com

About the Illustrator

ELISHA GILLETTE is an artist who learned to draw by watching a lot of behind-the-scenes features on their favorite DVDs. Since going to the Rhode Island School of Design, they have called Providence home, though they miss their friends and family back in hometown San Mateo, California. They are currently having a blast making art for books, tabletop and video games, independent clients, and fellow nerds. When not drawing, Elisha is most often observed playing D&D, going on walks with their partner and puppies, crocheting, and baking strange desserts they found on the internet. Elisha loves a good cup of crysanthemum tea and talking to people about their stories.

🔊 www.elishagillette.art | elishagillette.carrd.co | ✉ elishagillette@gmail.com

Santa's Behavior Chart

Name _____   Date _____

I DO MY BEST TO...	FOR KIDS		FOR PARENTS	
	YES	NO	YES	NO
Be a Good Helper				
Be a Good Listener				
Be Kind				
Share Nicely with Others				
Keep Bedroom Clean				
Work Hard in School				
Always Be Honest				
Give Back to the Community				
Be Polite				
No Drama				
No Attitude				
Stay Safe and Healthy